Wild Cat

Written by Berlie Doherty

Illustrated by Zara Slattery

Collins

1 Beautiful creatures

Something strange was happening in
the valley where Catrin lived. When she
looked out of the window at night, she felt as if
something was out there on the dark mountain,
moving softly, watching.

Catrin was a bit of a dreamer, everyone said.
She didn't really mix with the other children in
the village, and she wasn't one for playing in
the park or going to friends' houses for parties
and sleepovers. It wasn't that she didn't like the
other children or that they didn't like her; she
was just what they called a loner, and people
accepted it.

She liked to read and draw best of all, and
she was passionate about anything to do with
animals. Nain, her grandmother, said she was
just like her father had been, at Catrin's age.
"And look at your father now, travelling
all over the world, making wildlife films
for TV!" Nain said proudly. "Maybe you'll
do something like that one day, Catrin!"

Catrin couldn't imagine it. She couldn't imagine going anywhere outside her own valley, for a start; her beautiful green valley, with its winding river and its dark, towering mountains. Dad was always off somewhere, filming penguins in the South Pole, turtles in Zanzibar or lions in Kenya. Mum was his researcher, finding out about all the different species and their habitats to help Dad with his work.

"One day," Mum used to say, "I'm going to go with you, Gareth. You have all the fun!"

"Are you really, Mum?" Catrin would ask, worried.

"Not yet," Mum promised. "Not till you're bigger. But one day, I will. I really want to."

When Catrin was 11, Mum decided she was actually going to do it. Dad had been asked to go to South China to film tigers, and when they talked to Catrin about it, Mum's eyes shone with excitement.

"This is it!" Mum said. "This is the one I really want to do!"
She looked at Catrin. "What do you think?" she asked.
"If I go with Dad, what would you think?"

Catrin frowned. She wasn't sure what to think. She'd never
seen her mother looking so pleased and excited.

"Tigers, Catrin!"

In spite of herself, Catrin felt a shiver of excitement. Dad had always told her that tigers were the most beautiful creatures on the earth, muscular and powerful, gold and black like sunlight rippling through the branches of trees.

"Will it be dangerous?"

"Oh no. We'd be with local guides," Mum assured her.

"It's important that we do this," Dad explained. "It's very rare to see one in the wild now. Tigers are very, very much endangered everywhere. You know that, don't you?"

Catrin nodded. "They might become extinct," she whispered. Even as she said it, she felt the sharp sting of tears. How could tigers disappear for ever? It was unthinkable.

"And most of all in South China. No one has seen a tiger in those mountains for over 20 years. It could be that they'll never be seen there again." He went very quiet for a moment. "We want to try to see one, Catrin. Before they all disappear. We want to film them, to show the world how beautiful these creatures are."

"Am I coming with you?"

And then Dad stroked Catrin's hair in that special way he had when she was worried or upset, and said, "No, my love. We can't take you. What about school? I might be away for months!"

"*I'm* just going to stay there for a month," Mum promised. "That's not long, is it?"

"When will you be going?" Catrin could hear a wail of despair rising in her voice.

"Not yet. We need to have our injections, sort out our visas for China, work out our route and Dad's schedule. It'll take ages yet."

"I wish there were tigers here, in Wales," Catrin said. "Then we could all see them, and you wouldn't have to go away."

"But there aren't," Dad said. "And that's the point. If we're going to see them at all, we have to take this job."

"Have a think about it," said Mum. "I really want to go, Catrin. But I won't go unless I know you're happy about it."

Happy about it! How could I be? Catrin thought, but she didn't say anything. She just sat staring at Dad's wildlife photographs on the walls. She knew them all so well that she sometimes felt as if the animals of the jungles and mountains were as familiar as the sheep and cows in the fields outside the window. *Soon,* she thought, *there might be one of a tiger, and it would be the best photograph of all. How could she say anything to stop her parents from going? Especially when Mum was so excited and happy?* Mum was still talking about her plans, but Catrin had stopped listening. She was imagining herself walking stealthily up the side of a mountain in South China, crouching behind rocks, peering into caves, listening with every nerve of her body for the sound of a tiger breathing.

"We've had an idea about the house,"
Mum said, and Catrin turned sharply to look
at her, startled back into the present.
"When we go, if we go, we thought
we might rent out the house for a month or so."

Catrin stared at her. "Our house? Why?"

"When I was in Liverpool last week,
at Auntie Jean's, I met a family who are
moving into the new housing estate they're
building near your school. They've got
a boy about your age, and they'd like him
to start at your school as soon as the new
term begins, so I thought they could live in
our house till theirs is ready."

"No, please don't!" said Catrin,
panicking.

"They're really nice," Mum laughed.
"You'd like them."

"I don't care! I don't care what
they're like! I don't want them to come!"
Catrin burst out. She turned away, screwing
up her fists into tight little painful balls.
"I don't want to live with strangers."

Dad put his arms around her and held her close. "Oh, Catrin! You wouldn't be here! You'd be staying with Nain."

"With Nain!" Catrin smiled up at him, her eyes bright. She felt as if all her worry and panic had drifted away like the mist that rolled down the mountain. Her grandmother, Nain, was the best person in the world, after Mum and Dad. "She's as warm as toast," Dad often said. "As comfy as an old sofa." It was true. Sometimes, she was even better than Mum and Dad.

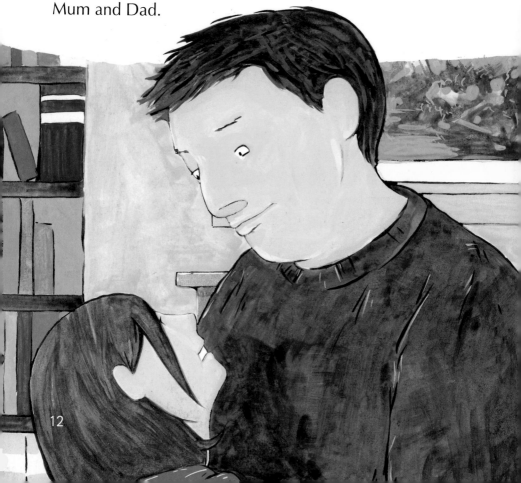

"There you are! Sunshine again!" Mum laughed.
"You'd like that, wouldn't you?"

"You'd be sleeping in my old bedroom," Dad said.
"It's just like yours, isn't it? So it wouldn't feel any different.
And I'd leave you a special present. I won't tell you what
it is. When you find it, you'll know."

"So, what do you say?" Mum asked.

"All right," said Catrin. "I think it's all right."

2 "It's too late."

Nain's house was right next door to Catrin's in the little row
of terraced houses by the river. The bedroom that Catrin
was moving into was just like her own, looking out towards
the highest of the mountains that stretched their bony arms
around the valley. She loved this mountain best of all.
She'd never climbed to the top, but she and Mum and Dad
often walked up the stony footpath to where a waterfall
streamed like the long, white tail of a wild horse.

Her dad told her that he had looked out at the same
mountain when he was a boy, and how he'd listened to
the mewing of the buzzards that lived high up on the crags.
"It was living here that made me love wild things," he said.
"Just like you do. We're very lucky."

"I know," said Catrin. "I'm never going to leave here."

Christmas that year seemed particularly special.
On Christmas Day they took a picnic up to the waterfall,
and sat huddled together against the biting wind, eating
cheese sandwiches and mince pies. They would have their
Christmas dinner with Nain that night, but this was special,
just for them.

From high up on the mountain came a shuddering, echoing moan.

"Did you hear that?" Catrin asked.

"It's the wind in the boulders," Mum said. "Eerie, isn't it?"

"Look at our valley stretched out below us," Dad said. "And the mountain towering above us. It's all ours today. There's no one else around, everything you see, everything you hear, even the wind on our cheeks, it's all just ours."

"Because everyone else is sensibly tucked up in front of a warm fire," Mum laughed.

"Ours, and the animals'," Catrin said dreamily. "It's their mountain too."

When the day came for Mum and Dad to go, Mum helped Catrin to pack the clothes and books and drawing pads she might need while she was at her grandmother's, and they locked the rest of her things away in the wardrobe. It felt strange to think that somebody else would be sleeping in her room that night. And it felt stranger still to be saying goodbye to Mum and Dad, even though she was used to the idea by now.

The taxi driver waited patiently while Catrin and Mum hugged each other. They were both half laughing, half crying.

"I'll be back before you know it!" Mum promised. "We'll phone as often as we can, but sometimes it won't be possible, when we're in really wild places."

Catrin nodded. She was used to that, when Dad went away.

"And we'll bring you lots of photographs of tigers, we hope."

Catrin smiled bravely. "Just don't get eaten by one, that's all."

"Look after her, Nain." And then they were gone. Catrin stood on the doorstep with Nain's arm around her shoulders, waving goodbye until the taxi disappeared from sight, until the sound of it had dropped away to nothing.

"We'll have a lovely time together," Nain said. She wiped her eyes and handed Catrin the tissue. "I can't believe how lucky I am, having my Catrin to stay with me. I think the time will go too quickly! You pop your bags upstairs and I'll get supper ready, and then we'll have a quiet walk by the river, if you like, before it gets dark. I love to watch the birds coming down to roost, don't you?"

Catrin went upstairs to her room and unpacked the last of her things into the drawers and on the shelves. The walls were still covered with drawings and photographs that Dad had made of animals in the fields of the valley; rabbits and hares, foxes and badgers. She smiled happily. The rooms in her own house next door were full of photographs of exotic animals like elephants and lions and rhinos, but really, Dad was right. She was completely at home here.

She was still unpacking when the family who were renting her house arrived. She could hear them moving around, talking, opening and closing drawers and cupboards to put away their own things. She could hear her bedroom window being opened, and a boy's voice saying, "There's just a big mountain, that's all."

That's all! Can't he see how beautiful the valley is, and all the different colours of the fields? She closed her own window quickly. She didn't want to think of anyone else being in her room. And would he sense what she sensed at night, she wondered? Would he have the feeling that something was coming down from the mountain, watching and waiting, silent as shadows?

She ran downstairs quickly, trying to shake the night thoughts away. "Nain, the new people have come," she said.

"I know. I saw them. The boy will be in your class at school. Isn't that nice! And you'll be able to talk English to him, because you speak it better than anyone else."

Catrin said nothing. She opened up her sketch pad and began to draw a tiger, copying from a book that Mum had left for her.

Nain left her to it, but much later, she said, "Just think, Catrin. Everybody's happy! The English family get somewhere to live, your mum gets to go on the trip of her dreams, and I get my lovely Catrin to live with me! It's wonderful." She looked anxiously at Catrin. "You are happy about it, aren't you?"

Catrin nodded, but she couldn't say anything. She didn't want to hurt Nain's feelings, but now that the excitement of packing and unpacking was over, along with looking at maps with Mum and Dad, tracing their route, laughing with Mum about the mosquito net on her trekking hat; now that Mum had really gone, she felt empty and flat.

"The time will fly, you'll see," said Nain. "Mum and Dad will be back soon, with all their stories."

"I know, Nain. It's all right."

Nain sighed. "You wish it was you, don't you, going to find a tiger? When you're older, you can do things like that."

Catrin nodded again. Her throat was tight. What if all
the tigers had gone by then? And the thought that Dad
might be right, and that soon there might be no tigers left
in the world, made her want to cry.

And there was something else that she was
unhappy about. She didn't like the thought of other
people living in her house, sleeping in their beds, sitting at
their table. Most of all, she didn't like the boy who was
using her room, because he didn't like the mountain.
And she certainly didn't want to have to talk English to him,
just because he didn't speak Welsh. She didn't want to
have to talk to him at all. She carried on drawing, biting
her lip with concentration, glancing at the book and back
at her page, shading and colouring, getting it right.
Nain hummed to herself and carried on making supper.
Perhaps she knew what Catrin was really feeling.

24

"Did you have a really good look around your room?" she asked. "Your dad told me you'd find something special, somewhere. Wouldn't tell me what it was. He said you'd know it was for you when you found it. So I haven't gone prying! All I've done is make up your bed and pop a hot water bottle inside it. By the way, did you find anything? Why don't you have another look? And when you come down we'll have that walk, and then a piece of cake with supper, shall we?"

Catrin put her tiger drawing to one side and went upstairs, just to please Nain. She looked in the drawers, in the wardrobe, behind the curtains on the windowsill, but Catrin really couldn't find anything. Perhaps, whatever it was, Dad had forgotten to leave it there.

"Well, if he's forgotten, he'll remember, and he'll post it to you," Nain said.

"He left me all his photographs," Catrin said. "Maybe that's it."

"Oh, those photographs!" Nain laughed and shook her head. "I don't know, what a child he was! He was always taking photographs. He loved animals and birds so much, Catrin! He had a little menagerie full of animals he'd found. A grass snake, a starling with one white wing, little orphan robins. Oh, but it's changed a lot around here, even since he was a boy. There aren't as many birds here as there used to be. The fields were full of them, the trees were full of them, the sky was full of them. There's many a bird I don't see these days, that I remember from when I was a child, like the red kite. And I don't hear the skylark now, and it used to fill the summer sky with sweetness. And as for animals – I haven't seen a deer since I don't know when."

"Why is that, Nain? Why don't they come any more?"

"Well, they say it's the way people farm these days, and the way houses are built on places that were special to some of these creatures. Barns are converted into houses, walls and hedges are taken down to make bigger fields. Look at that new estate that's being built now."

"That's where the boy in my room is going to live."

"I know. Three or four fields were there before, and a lovely copse of ash and chestnut trees. What happened to the creatures that used to live there? The mice and the squirrels and the badgers? The owls? Just think, nowhere for them to roost or nest or sleep. The food they eat isn't there any more, so they have to go somewhere else for it. And of course, foxes aren't welcome. Farmers hate foxes, and I understand why, because they eat the young chicks – but oh, my heart still stops for a moment when I see one streaking across the fields!"

"Me too!" smiled Catrin. "Dad told me that there used to be wild animals up in the mountain."

Nain laughed. "Oh, he used to tell me that too! Well, there are buzzards; you still see them. And hares that turn white in winter. Lovely, aren't they? But your father said there was a deep, dark cave up there, right at the top, where a wild cat used to live."

"A wild cat!" Catrin could hardly breathe. She felt her heart thudding in her throat. "A wild cat, like a tiger?"

"A lot smaller than a tiger! Not much bigger than my old Stripes. But wild all the same, truly wild. Your father went up there a few times to try to find it, but he never did. I told him, wild cats don't live here any more. They're extinct in these parts. But he didn't believe me. Didn't want to." She sighed. "No, he has to go all the way to China if he wants to see anything as wild as that."

"Wild cats!" Catrin said again. "Did you ever see one, Nain?"

"Oh, I might have done. Many, many years ago. But I can't be sure."

"I would love to see one!" Catrin sighed. "A real wild cat!"

"I'm sorry, Catrin," Nain said, "they've all gone. It's too late."

That night Catrin opened her bedroom window wide and looked out into the starry darkness. The mountain loomed behind the village, darker than the night sky. But nothing moved. Nothing.

"Wild cat!" she whispered. "I wish you were there!"

3 Out of the gloomy dusk there came a howl

On the first day of the new term, the English
boy's mother brought him to the school.
He stood next to the teacher, Mrs Thomas,
smiling bravely at everyone as if he had known
them all his life, while Mrs Thomas introduced
him to the class.

"This is Leo," she said. "He doesn't speak any
Welsh, but he's going to learn with me, aren't
you, Leo? We'll still have most of our lessons
in Welsh, children, but I expect you to help
Leo as much as you can. And of course, we
have someone who can be very helpful indeed,
because she speaks English just as well as she
speaks Welsh. So, Catrin, move your chair along.
Leo can sit next to you."

Catrin went scarlet. This was even worse
than she'd imagined. She moved her chair as far
away from the boy as she could. He sat down,
still smiling. If he felt scared at the thought of
being in a new school and having to learn a new
language, he didn't show it.

At playtime he sat on the wall like Catrin, but neither of them spoke to each other. He watched the other children eagerly as they ran around, shouting and laughing. He was keen to join in if they'd let him, but he didn't understand their language, and he wasn't quite brave enough to run up to them. Most of the other children could speak a bit of English, but Welsh came more easily to them, and they didn't think to spare the time to talk to him in his language. So he and Catrin sat at opposite ends of the wall every playtime, just forgotten about. She'd be daydreaming or drawing and he'd be listening, listening hard, trying to make sense of everything.

At lunchtime and after school the two teachers took it in turns to give Leo Welsh lessons, but it would be a long time before he knew enough to be able to understand properly. It was very hard for him. Catrin was too shy to speak English to him, even though Mrs Thomas asked her to help. "Catrin, your English is much better than mine! Come and help me out!"

But Catrin blushed till her face was burning, and kept her head down, and Mrs Thomas didn't ask her again. She was used to Catrin's shyness.

It was probably because she had such a quietness
inside her that Catrin sensed that something peculiar was
happening around the village. At first it was just the feeling at
night, the sense that something was outside on the mountain,
watching and waiting. And then, a few days after she moved
to Nain's, she heard something: a strange, lost cry, coming
from way up in the dark purple mountain. Wondering about
the cry kept her awake at night. It made her restless and
anxious, a bit fluttery inside. Once she'd heard it, she found
she was listening for it all the time. She lay watching the
moon rising and setting; she heard the birds settling down
to sleep, crooning in their roosts.

Every morning, she heard the slow dawn chorus, as
one by one the birds woke up and filled the air with song.
Day after night and night after day, she watched and
listened, and the more she did this, the more sure she was
that something was different. It was almost as if the birds
were listening too. But she never spoke a word about it
to anyone. She kept her thoughts churning around inside
herself. She kept gazing out of the window, as if she was
watching for something, as if she was straining to hear
something that no one else could hear.

But then, one sleepy afternoon in school, the new boy, Leo, started so suddenly that his chair shrieked like a seagull. He looked quickly around the classroom to see if anyone else had heard what he'd heard. All the other children were scribbling away at their work, and Mrs Thomas was marking books. Only Catrin, he noticed, was staring out of the window, alert, listening too with every nerve of her body. Her eyes caught his, and she looked down quickly. But she held her breath. The English boy had also heard it. She wasn't imagining it. Something was out there.

A storm was brewing that afternoon, as the children were leaving school. The sky was heavy with thunder-black clouds, and the mountains surrounding the valley were midnight dark. Suddenly out of the gloom there came a howl that sent shivers down everybody's spine.

"What on earth was that?" Mrs Thomas said.

"Just a storm," said the infant teacher, Mrs Jones. "But it's very fierce and that rain is coming down heavily, so everyone should go straight home." She put on her coat to go to her own house, and then they heard the howl again, echoing down from the mountains. The children clamoured around Mrs Jones, shouting each other down.

39

"It's not the storm, Miss, it's a wolf," said Bethan.

"It's a leopard!" said Ellie.

"A lynx!"

"It's a tiger!"

"Don't be silly," Mrs Jones said. "We don't have any of those sorts of animals in this country. It's just the storm, get home quickly."

The children did as they were told, but they were calling to each other excitedly as they went, making howling noises and curling their hands like claws. They shrieked and wailed down the dim streets, scared and excited.

Leo and Catrin walked side by side to their houses. At first neither of them said anything, then Leo spoke, "Have you heard it before? Before today, I mean?"

Catrin nodded.

"Lots of times?"

"Last night. And the night before," she said. "A few times."

"Do you think it's coming from the mountain?" he asked.

She nodded again.

"I do too." And when he reached his door, he paused, with his hand on the doorknob. "What do you think it is?"

"I *know* what it is," she said. She paused, not sure for a moment whether to tell him or not. "It's a wild cat!"

4 There's a wild animal out there!

For a few days nothing happened – and then it came again,
that chilling, lonely howl. It seemed to go on all night
this time. It was as if everyone was aware of something now,
and couldn't stop talking about it, wondering and guessing.
And it splintered into their heads and crept into their very
bones, until it began to haunt their dreams. Soon there
were all kinds of stories being told about a strange, wild
creature from the mountain.

"Mrs Jenkins saw it," Ellis and Ellie's mother announced.
"She was bringing in the
washing, and there it was
in her own back yard!
It's the size of
a sheep, with yellow
eyes like torches!"

A man said his
brother had seen
it running in the
headlights of his car.
"It was as golden as the sun,"
he said. "A beautiful creature."

Some people who knew somebody who'd seen it heard that it was a ghostly thing with moon-white skin and glowing coals for eyes, but others said no, it was as black and silent as shadows. Someone had seen it running along rooftops, and leaping through open windows. And as the days went on, the stories grew wilder: it had killed a dog, mauled sheep, taken the hens, eaten a rabbit's head, and shredded a goose. Someone from another valley altogether said it had attacked a horse.

And all this time, the children of the village were getting more and more excited. When school was over they ran home, their high voices echoing down the alleys and bouncing off the house walls. Their mothers called them in from the streets and kept them inside their houses.

"You mustn't go out in the dark!" they were told. "There's a wild animal out there!"

One day, Catrin and Leo both stayed on after school. Leo was having his Welsh lesson with Mrs Thomas, and Catrin was finishing off some drawings for a display. After his lesson, Leo came into the classroom with his books.

Then it came again, sudden as lightning: that sad, strange, lonely cry.

"Wild cat!" Catrin whispered. "Did you hear it?"

Leo nodded, holding his breath. He stared down at Catrin's pictures. They were all of wild cats, stripy creatures with thick tails, hissing, arching their backs, pricking up their sharp ears.

"They're really good," Leo said. "How do you know it looks like that?"

"I just think it does," Catrin said, blushing sharply.

"I tried to draw one, but it just looked like a fat old tabby cat! I'm going to get some books from the library bus, and find out about it," Leo said. He picked up his bag. "D'you want to come with me?"

Catrin shook her head, not looking at him.

"Do you know what?" Leo said. "We've both got cat names. Catrin and Leo. I think we're meant to find out about the wild cat, don't you?"

Catrin said nothing. She gathered up her pictures and put them in a folder.

"What are you going to do with the pictures?"

"Mrs Thomas asked me to do them," she told him shyly. "But I might stick some up on my bedroom wall." *If there's room,* she thought. *I'd have to take some of Dad's down to do that. He mightn't like it.* "I want to show them to my dad when he comes home. But maybe he won't be interested in things like that any more. Not now that he's looking for tigers in China."

"Leo and Catrin," Mrs Thomas called. "You go home now. It's late."

"Is he really? Looking for tigers?"

Catrin nodded. "And my mum is with him."

"Tell you what I'm going to do," Leo whispered. "I'm going to look for the wild cat! Up in the mountain! Will you come?"

Catrin couldn't speak at first. She wanted to find the wild cat, more than anything else. But what would Nain say? She knew very well. Nain would say no.

So she shook her head. "No," she said, although she wanted to say yes more than anything else in the world. "I don't think so." And she ran home, alone.

5 Special things

"You've just missed your mum and dad on the phone," Nain told her when she arrived at the house.

"Have they seen a tiger?"

"No. Not yet. But they think they've found his tracks. Your mum was so excited. They're going to follow the tracks tomorrow, she said. Just think, those tracks might lead them to a real tiger!"

Just after they'd finished their supper, Leo knocked on the door, with some books tucked under his arm.

Nain invited him in, but Catrin jumped up to go to
her room.

"Catrin, here's your friend," Nain said. "Clear a space for
him on the sofa and perk up the fire. You've brought all
the cold air in with you, boy! You must be freezing!"

"No, I'm roasting!" he told her. His cheeks were hot and
red, and his breath was bursting from him. He'd obviously
run all the way home from the library bus, straight to
Catrin's house. "I've been finding out about the wild cat,"
he said.

Nain smiled and went into the kitchen to wash up.

Leo knelt down on the carpet and flicked open the pages. "Look at it! Just like your drawings! And d'you know what, I've found out that they've been around longer than we have! I mean, longer than any humans! Just think. It's only little, not much bigger than a domestic cat, but it's really, really wild. It doesn't need humans at all."

Catrin traced the shape of the photograph with her fingers, measuring the size of the cat's head against its body. "Look at its long, thick tail!" she said. "I didn't get that right. And its ears are really big and sharp!"

Leo knelt back. "We've got to see it. It must be up there."

"It is," said Catrin firmly.

"I'm definitely going to go. It'll have to be Saturday, because it's too dark after school. This Saturday. Will you come, Catrin? You have to come! I don't know my way up the mountain."

"I don't really either," she whispered back. "I only know as far as the waterfall."

"Then let's go there, and look for tracks! If we find tracks, we'll know that the wild cat still exists here!"

"Like Mum and Dad have done," Catrin said. "They've found tiger tracks."

"Please, Catrin! Say you will!"

But Catrin shook her head. She still didn't want to show Leo her special path to the waterfall, her favourite walk with Mum and Dad. She was too shy to share it with him.

Disappointed, he picked up his library books. "Well then. I'll go on my own," he said. And when Nain came in with hot cakes and strawberry jam, he shook his head, said goodnight to them both and went home.

"Well, and I thought you'd made a friend at last,"
Nain sighed.

"He's not my friend," Catrin said. "I don't need a friend."
She went up to her room and spread out her drawings on
the bed. She would put two up, she decided, there's just
enough room. And she could store the others under
the bed in a folder until Mum and Dad came home.

She chose one of the wild cat on a boulder. It was
snarling, ears flattened, back bent to spring at something.
She liked that because it made the wild cat look just as wild
as any tiger or lion she'd seen in a picture. And she chose
another of the wild cat slinking through grass, its legs long
and its muscles taut, and its ears pricked high to catch
the sound of any creature.

Nain came in to admire them. She folded her arms and
shuddered. "My, I wouldn't want to be attacked by that
one!" she said. "It's very
scary, Catrin. Scary and
beautiful."

Catrin smiled.
That was exactly what
she had wanted to show
in her drawings: a wild,
fierce beauty.

She bent down to slide the folder of drawings under the bed, but it knocked against something small and hard. She groped under the bed and pulled out a wooden box.

"Good heavens!" Nain gasped. "I haven't seen that for years!"

"What is it?"

"It's your father's box of special things! Well, I might have known that was where he'd hide it, under his bed. Open it, Catrin! That's your present. It's yours now."

It was an old oblong case like a large pencil case, with a little notch on the lid. Catrin dipped her finger into the notch and slid back the lid. Inside were a tooth, a feather, and a long bony thing, a bit like a comb.

"Oh, he used to love those!" Nain said. "Do you know what they are? The tooth of a fox, the feather of an eagle, the spine of a fish. He found them all. Every time he went on an adventure, he used to take them with him, for luck."

The next day was Saturday. Catrin could hear Leo moving about in his room next door, pulling open the drawer of his cupboard, running up and down the stairs. She could tell that he was excited, and she knew why. She went downstairs and ate her breakfast in silence, watching the kitchen window, which opened into the street. But there was no sign of Leo leaving the house. *He's changed his mind,* she thought. *He's too scared to go.*

As she tidied her room and made her bed, she kept glancing out of the window. Still no sign of Leo. *Perhaps he went the other way up the street,* she thought. *He's gone the wrong way. He'll never find it now!*

It was late morning, and she was helping Nain to peel potatoes, when at last she heard Leo's front door opening, heard him shouting, "Bye, Mum! See you later." She saw his brown hair bobbing as he ran past her window.

She couldn't bear it any longer. She scraped back her chair and ran to the front door and out into the street. There he was, just about to turn the corner. He'd missed the gate that would lead him to the track up the mountain. "Leo! Leo!" she shouted. "It's the wrong way!"

For a moment she thought he hadn't heard her, or didn't want to. Then he turned and just stood there with his hands spread out as if to say, so what do I do? And she made up her mind.

"Wait for me! I'm coming with you!" She rushed back into the house and up the stairs to her room, rooted under her bed and pulled out her father's box of lucky things.

She skidded down the stairs again, and out of the house into the street. Leo was still there, waiting for her.

"Let's go!" he said, grinning.

"Let's find the wild cat!" Catrin added back.

She couldn't remember feeling so happy.

6 Follow the track

"So which way do we go?" Leo asked.

"Through the farm gate. It's all right, we always go that way. Then we follow the track that the badgers use."

"Badgers! I've never seen a badger."

Catrin looked around the field. "See that hole below the wall up there, with a pile of earth scuffed in front of it? That's the entrance to a badger sett. It's quite new, that one."

Leo ran to the hole and crouched down on his hands and knees, peering down it. "Can't see anything."

"You won't. They don't come out till dusk. Anyway, it's a wild cat we're after, not a badger."

He stood up, brushing the earth from his hands and his jeans. "OK. Lead on."

Catrin moved away, shy and proud and thrilled. She felt like one of the local guides that Mum and Dad would be using in China.

"Now we start to climb up," she said. "It's a bit steep at first, and then it levels out and you start to hear the water trickling. And then … up there, where there's a holly tree – can you see it? Bright red berries?"

Leo nodded.

"We go on to a ledge just past it, and we'll see the waterfall. And we don't stop till we get there."

That was what Dad always said. She was glad now that she was taking Leo there, after all. It was fine.

It was one of those cold, bright, sharp winter days. The sun was in their eyes as they climbed towards the waterfall. It was hard going, and took them much longer than they expected. Below them they could see the village spread out, the streets and the school, the church, the new houses, the sparkle of the river winding around it, and beyond that, the fields. As they reached the waterfall, a brisk wind tossed the spray upwards, so it showered them with fine, cold splinters of icy water, making them both scream with laughter. Catrin wondered what Mum would say if she could hear her now.

"Shh!" Catrin said suddenly. "We mustn't make a noise, or we'll frighten the wild cat away. We must keep very still and quiet now. Dad says you have to be as still as a stone before a wild animal will come near you."

"I've brought some sandwiches. Perhaps if we eat one, it'll be tempted down by the smell," Leo suggested.

"We'll share one," Catrin whispered. "But be very slow and still. No sudden movements."

"We should hunt for tracks."

"Not yet!" Catrin whispered. "Keep still for a bit."

Leo stared at her. The expedition had been his idea, after all. But he said nothing, just carefully broke a sandwich into two halves and very, very slowly lifted his piece to his mouth. Some crumbs of cheese rolled on to the ground. *Good,* he thought. *That's good bait.*

After a while, Catrin started to look around her. The ground beneath their feet was hard with frost, and just a few scruffy tufts of grass poked through. She stood up slowly and walked around to the edge of the little shelf above the waterfall, and Leo did the same.

"There's nothing, is there?" he whispered.

"Not a sign," Catrin agreed. She couldn't keep the disappointment out of her voice. They both looked up to where the track narrowed and wound its way up, around the back of the mountain, away from the village. The sun had moved, and was striking the snow on the upper levels with bright silver light. They both had the same thought at once.

"That's where the tracks will be," Catrin said.

"In the snow!"

They looked at each other, eyes shining again.

"It's not that far," said Leo, sensing that Catrin might not want to go any further. "It's about 15 minutes away, I'd guess."

"Just to the snow line, that's all."

"And as soon as we find the wild cat tracks, we'll come back down."

"We'll have to, before the sun goes."

Leo broke one of the other sandwiches and handed half to Catrin, and started to run forward.

"Leo!" she hissed.

He stopped. She put her finger to her lips.

"Sorry. I forgot," he whispered.

Very slowly and stealthily they began to move forward, glancing this way and that to see if they could catch sight of any movement, any track, anything to tell them that a creature was there.

A raven flung itself from a boulder, croaking its loud harsh cry, and they both jumped in fright. They inched forwards, slowly, slowly, their breath held in their throats, their lungs bursting. They would round one bend, and the path would snake tantalisingly out of sight behind boulders, rise a bit and then fall again. Catrin kept glancing back nervously. *As long as we keep the spray of the waterfall in sight,* she thought, *we're all right. We can't get lost.* Soon the path started climbing steeply upwards. They had to use both hands, and Leo slipped and grazed his knee on some boulders.

"That's it," said Catrin. "We have to stop now. It's getting dangerous."

"No, it isn't!" Leo said. "It isn't even hurting. And look, there's the snow. We've nearly reached it."

Panting, they scrambled up the last bit of stony path to where a powdering of snow shimmered around them. But there were no tracks to be seen. They stood with their hands on their hips, gazing around them, breath heaving. Nothing had walked across that snow, and it'd been there for weeks.

"What now?" Leo asked. But he knew the answer.

"We have to go home," Catrin said. Her voice was catching in her throat. "Perhaps Nain was right after all. There is no wild cat."

"And my knee hurts," Leo said in a small voice. He rolled his trouser leg up and looked at the slow trickle of blood seeping down his shin.

"Here." Catrin fished a tissue out of her pocket and dabbed at the graze. "We should've stopped when you fell. We shouldn't have come this far. And look." She turned around. "The sun's going behind the mountains. That means it'll be dusk soon, down in the valley. We'll have to hurry or everyone will be really worried or angry. Or both."

She looked anxiously to where the sun was dipping behind the mountain, its red light so fierce that it made her eyes hurt. Clouds that looked heavy with snow bunched up. She knew they had to go home. All the excitement of the morning had fizzled away. She yearned to go on and up, right up, to the cave at the top of the mountain. It was almost unbearable to have come so far, to have seen no sign of the wild cat, and to have to turn back home.

"The cave," Leo whispered. "Catrin, we have to go to the cave to see if the wild cat is there. We can't go back now."

Up there, where the snow was deep, where the buzzards soared, where the white hares lived, that was where the wild cat must be. If it existed at all. She knew Leo was right – they had to look.

She said nothing, but climbed on grimly, her breath bursting from her in sharp painful gasps, and close behind her Leo struggled and panted. It began to snow; soft, light flakes that covered their tracks in seconds. It was hopeless, she knew it was hopeless, yet she couldn't stop now.

At last they were as high as they could go, and there was the cave, like a huge, black, open mouth, yawning in front of them.

They paused. Leo slipped off his backpack and lowered it on to a boulder soundlessly, easing the ache in his shoulders. He gestured to Catrin. *Now!* his eyes said.

They went in together, on tiptoe, breath held.

Nothing. Nothing was there.

Catrin walked out of the cave thinking about her father's box of special things. She turned to Leo to see if he was following her, and in that split second, that was when she saw it.

There was a sudden, stealthy movement, as soft as a breath.

The wild cat slinked soundlessly out from behind the boulder where Leo had put his backpack. The wind must have been blowing their voices and their scent away from the wild cat, because it was just as surprised as Catrin was. It stood stock-still, one paw lifted, ears pricked, eyes huge. It was staring straight at Catrin.

Leo saw the amazed look on her face, turned, and his sudden movement startled the wild cat into life. With a bound it was away and out of sight; all Leo saw was the dark flash that was the thick bush of its tail.

7 "I saw it!"

"I saw it!" Catrin felt as if she hadn't breathed for at least five minutes. "I saw it! It is! It is! It's the wild cat!"

"I saw it too!" said Leo. "I saw its tail. I saw the wild cat's tail!"

"It was so beautiful! It stared right at me! I couldn't breathe! I thought I was going to burst!"

They couldn't stop talking now, laughing and shouting to each other as they scurried and skidded their way back down the mountain. Snow buffeted their faces, clung to their eyelashes, and they didn't care.

"We saw the wild cat!"

"We saw the wild cat!"

"It would've been good if we'd had a camera," Leo said. "We could've shown a photograph of the wild cat to everyone at school."

"No, it wouldn't," said Catrin slowly. "Just think – if they knew it was here, they'd all want to come up and see it."

"They might scare it away."

"Shall we not tell anyone?"

"It's our secret. Our special secret."

"Not even Nain? And Dad?"

Leo thought for a bit. "I think you should tell them," he said at last. "I think they'd want to keep it a secret too."

Nain was watching anxiously from the window. As soon as she saw the children coming, she opened the door and stood on the doorstep with her hands on her hips.

"Where on earth have you been all this time?" she asked. "It's almost dark! I've been worried sick, and your parents are too, Leo."

"I'm sorry," said Leo. "It was my fault really. It was my idea."

"Go on in to your mam," Nain said. "You've got some explaining to do, young man."

For a second Leo and Catrin looked at each other and exchanged grins. Then he slipped past her and into his own house, and Nain ushered Catrin into theirs, shutting the door firmly behind her.

"We didn't mean to be late," Catrin said. "We went to find wild cat tracks, up by the waterfall."

"Did you now!" Nain snorted. "And did you find any?"

"No," said Catrin. She wasn't looking at Nain. She held her head down. "We didn't find any tracks near the waterfall, so we went up to the snow line to find some. We thought it was only 15 minutes away, but it was much further."

"An hour further, at least," said Nain. "I'm very cross with you. Go and get your coat and boots off, and get yourself warm by the fire."

"And Leo hurt his knee, and I cleaned it for him. That took a few minutes."

Nain grunted again. She closed the door and drew the curtains. It was nearly dark outside.

"And then we went up to the cave."

"Right to the top? In this weather!"

"Nain," Catrin whispered. "We saw it. The wild cat. We really saw it."

Nain turned around, shaking her head. "You can't have done."

"You told me I must never lie. I'm telling you the truth. We saw it."

Nain came over to her granddaughter and held her at arm's length, a hand on each of her shoulders. She looked into her bright, happy face, and then pulled her close and hugged her tight. "That's wonderful. That's so wonderful, my Catrin."

That night, when she was in bed, Catrin lay in the darkness, wondering. Had she seen it? Or had she imagined it? But how could she have imagined the feeling of wonder and excitement, the shiver of fear and the utter, overwhelming joy she'd felt when the wild cat had stared straight into her eyes?

And then, just as she was drifting away on the warm tide of a memory that would never leave her, she heard something: a long, sad, lonely cry, from somewhere up in the black mountain. She turned over in her bed, smiled, and went to sleep.

Catrin's roles

dreamer

artist

animal lover

friend

loner

adventurer

leader

explorer

79

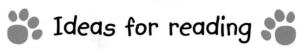

Ideas for reading

Written by Clare Dowdall BA(Ed), MA(Ed)
Lecturer and Primary Literacy Consultant

Learning objectives: understand underlying themes, causes and points of view; sustain engagement with longer texts using different techniques to make the text come alive; use the techniques of dialogic talk to explore ideas, topics or issues; improvise using a range of drama strategies and conventions to explore themes; use different narrative techniques to engage and entertain the reader; select words and language drawing on their knowledge of literary features and formal and informal writing

Curriculum links: Citizenship: Taking part; Geography: The mountain environment

Interest words: menagerie, mauled, tantalisingly

Resources: paper, pens, whiteboard

Getting started

This book can be read over two or more reading sessions.

- Explain that this story is about a wild mountain cat. Ask children if they know any myths about wild animals, e.g. The Dartmoor Beast, and discuss the characteristics they think a wild cat would have.

- Ask children to describe what the Welsh mountain landscape might be like, and how the setting might affect the story. Encourage them to use adjectives in their answers.

Reading and responding

- Ask children to read to p13, thinking about how they would feel if they were Catrin and their parents were going to China for two months.

- Ask children to continue reading to p31, focusing on the character of Catrin. Discuss what they know and can infer about her, e.g. *She doesn't feel that she needs friends because she is happy with her own company.*

- Ask children to continue reading the story, looking for examples of how the author is building tension in the story by using vivid description, e.g. *"It splintered into their heads and crept into their very bones, until it began to haunt their dreams."*